Bright Summaries.com

Witches

BY MONA CHOLLET

BOOK ANALYSIS

Written by Amandine Farges
Translated by Oliver Brown

Witches

BY MONA CHOLLET

WITCHES

ESSAY ON THE FIGURE OF THE WITCH, A FEMINIST ICON

- **Genre:** Essay

- **Reference edition:** *Sorcières. La puissance invaincue des femmes*, Paris, Éditions La Découverte Zones, 2018, 240 pages.

- **1st edition:** 2018

- **Themes:** feminism, patriarchy, motherhood, ageism, couple, ecofeminism

In September 2018, Zones, published by La Découverte, *Sorcières. La puissance invaincue des femmes*. In this essay, Mona Chollet establishes a link between the witch hunts that took place during the Renaissance and the manifestations of misogyny towards 'witches' in the modern era: the independent woman, the childless woman and the elderly woman.

Through a historical approach, but also modern references, even from pop culture, Mona Chollet analyses why free women are frightening and by what means patriarchal society has always wanted to repress them. For it is also a particular relationship to the world that is promoted by those who are similar to witches. By distancing themselves from the exploitation of nature by man, they invent ecofeminism.

Sorcières. La puissance invaincue des femmes, a bestseller that has sold 270,000 copies, is translated into 15 languages. It won the Prix de l'Essai Psychologies-Fnac in 2019.

MONA CHOLLET

SWISS WRITER

- **Born in 1973 in Geneva**

- **Some of his works:**

  - *Fatal Beauty. The New Faces of Female Alienation* (2015), essay

  - *At Home. An odyssey of domestic space* (2015), essay

  - *Reinventing Love: How patriarchy sabotages heterosexual relationships* (2021), essay

Born in Geneva to a Swiss father and an Egyptian mother, Mona Chollet studied modern literature and went on to attend the Lille School of Journalism. She is currently a journalist and editor at Le Monde diplomatique. She also runs the cultural criticism website *Périphéries*, in partnership with Thomas Lemahieu.

She is the author of several essays on the status of women, particularly through the various injunctions imposed on women: beauty, motherhood, marriage, etc.

Since *Sorcières. La puissance invaincue des femmes*, released in 2018, Mona Chollet is one of the most widely read feminists in France.

In 2021, her much-anticipated new essay, *Reinventing Love: How patriarchy sabotages heterosexual relationships*. It won the Les Inrockuptibles essay prize.

SUMMARY

Mona Chollet begins her text by evoking the fascination that the figure of the witch exerted on her as a child and for what reasons: 'Through her came the idea that being a woman could mean additional power, whereas until then a diffuse impression suggested to me that it was rather the opposite' (p.11).

WITCHES THROUGH THE AGES

In this long introduction of some forty pages, the author returns to those who have been called witches through the ages and especially to the hunts of which they were the object. While, in the collective unconscious, these hunts took place in the Middle Ages, in reality, it was during the Renaissance that they were the most violent and the most numerous (there is talk of a million victims). At that time, misogyny was important and any powerful woman, therefore irreducible to the role that society wanted to assign her, was suspected of hiding a demon within her: 'Talking back to a neighbour, speaking loudly, having a strong character or a sexuality that was a little too free, being a nuisance in any way was enough to put you in danger' (p.17). It is to bring these free women into line that the staging of their torments is invented.

Much later, as the 1970s examined these abuses, feminists defined themselves as the granddaughters of these witches, taking up the desire for emancipation and the attacks on them. Ecological concerns and the importance given to the living world also lead to the reappearance of the figure of the witch as a woman who is part of a world not yet exploited by the rationality and productivism of men.

Taking the figure of the witch as her object of reflection, Mona Chollet is interested in those who today hold the place of this 'woman freed from all dominations, all limitations' (p. 11). In the four parts of this book, the essayist aims to revisit the social and political constraints that weigh heavily on women, illustrating her point with examples of women authors who embody resistance to these prohibitions: figures of combatants in the face of the obstacles still erected in the face of women's desire for independence.

WOMEN'S INDEPENDENCE SEEN AS A DANGER

For example, while widows and unmarried women make up the bulk of those accused of witchcraft, even today 'the independence of women, even when legally possible, continues to be met with general scepticism' (p. 35).

The witch seems to be the only female archetype that defines itself without recourse to a male partner. It is only a short step from the witch of yesteryear to the mocked 'cat lady' of today. Yet a woman who does not define herself in relation to a dominant man is in fact a strong woman, as the luminous figure of Gloria Steinem admirably illustrates.

A WOMAN IS NOT NECESSARILY A MOTHER

On the other hand, the witch-hunt was based on the criminalisation of contraception and abortion. Witches were considered by all as 'anti-mothers'. This mistrust is reflected in our society today through the mistrust, even general disapproval, of childless women. Women who refuse to have children are thus confronted with the prejudice that they hate children or that they are just heartless egotists, which is never reproached to men without offspring.

It is so difficult to escape this injunction to desire children that some women give in to it, unconsciously repressing their deep desire and thus leading a life of dissatisfaction and even suffering.

BREAKING THE TABOO OF OLD AGE FOR WOMEN

Witch hunts have also instilled a very negative image of the old woman in people's minds. This vision is at work in the disgust inspired by women's white hair and the fact that a woman is supposed to age 'less well than a man'. It is also visible in the denial of female sexuality after a certain age.

> *It was the sexuality of older women that was particularly feared at the time. Since they no longer had a legitimate right to a sexual life, since they could no longer bear children and were sometimes widows, but were experienced and still desirable, they were seen as immoral and dangerous figures for the social order. (p.166)*

Many women authors have testified to the difficulty of being an old woman in contemporary society, of which they are not considered a full member. If a man gets older, it is not a problem, on the contrary, he gains in maturity, experience, even charm. Let a woman grow old and she loses her attractiveness. The fact that she too may gain in experience turns against her, because what is valued in a woman is never her power or her independence, but on the contrary her prettiness and her fragility, which a male partner can protect.

An older woman who is sure of her desires is often considered a "harpy".

FEMINISM AS A NEW RELATIONSHIP TO THE WORLD

Finally, Mona Chollet highlights the fact that the suspicion of witchcraft has largely targeted 'healers' and other women who used nature to heal their fellow human beings. As soon as man wanted to use his "rationality" to enslave nature according to his needs, any woman whose relationship to the world was not based on the exploitation of its riches became a witch. "The result was an arrogant science, nourished by contempt for the feminine, associated with the irrational, the sentimental, the hysterical, with a nature that had to be dominated" (p. 37).

This masculine position also leads to an intellectual insecurity for women, who are always referred to the realms of emotion, sensitivity and even simple affect.

The medical sector has also suffered from male pre-dominance, which has led to some mistreatment, especially of gynaecological patients, who are always suspected of 'making up stories, exaggerating, being ignorant, emotional and irrational' (p.202). Indeed, Mona Chollet concludes her text with a long list of the violence inflicted on women by medicine.

LIGHTING

Mona Chollet's book sets out to show that the criteria which, between the XV and XVII centuries, were used to make a woman a witch to be burned are still alive today. By studying the reactionary forces at work five centuries ago, she highlights those at work today, thus stimulating the feminist struggle underway and to come. "Tremble, the witches are coming back", said a feminist slogan from the 1970s. This is also what Mona Chollet seems to be shouting in her essay.

The author begins by looking at the witch hunts as a manifestation of misogyny, explaining that between the XV and XVII centuries, thousands of pyres were lit in Europe to destroy those seen as witches. According to statistics, 80% of the victims were women, especially elderly women. And while some men were accused of witchcraft, the vast majority were women who were prosecuted and subjected to inhuman torments, the only reasons being that they lived apart, did not give birth or did not attend church. Misogyny was therefore the primary reason for these atrocious persecutions.

And indeed, a hatred of women has been raging for centuries in Europe, successfully preparing the witch hunts that were unleashed during the Renaissance. Religion, science and justice combine to make women a demon to be destroyed. Assimilating women's bodies to a temptation, or even a danger for men, priests and doctors pointed the way to the stake.

The arts were not to be outdone in this period, where there are numerous examples, particularly in Baroque poetry, of detestation of women, and particularly of old women, often seen as demons. In his poem *Contre Denise sorcière* (*Against Denise the Witch*) in 1550, Pierre Ronsard addresses a long litany of insults to an old woman suspected of witchcraft (and whipped naked).

All the powers that be therefore converge to explain that women are bad.

By documenting the history of these 'witch hunts', Mona Chollet shows the extent to which men tried to cut off 'any female head that stuck out' (p.17), to annihilate any temptation of independence. Indeed, women are feared as soon as they are not submissive to their husbands, as soon as they do not sacrifice their lives to their children.

Whoever does not respond to these injunctions is suspect, say the men. Whoever does not respond to these injunctions is a feminist, replies Mona Chollet. In fact, even if the death penalty is no longer an issue, stigmatisation and violence against women do exist and it is these that the author wishes to denounce in this essay, which is at the heart of feminist thinking. The author paints several portraits of women who, not subordinated to a man, live autonomously, far from the norms imposed on their sex. Witches perhaps, feminists certainly.

The first feminist to take an interest in the history of witches and to claim the name herself was Matilda Joslyn Gage. This American woman (born in 1826 and died in 1898) campaigned for women's right to vote, thus continuing the line of 'witches' who were, no more and no less, independent women who wanted their full autonomy and fought to obtain it. It was Matilda Joslyn Gage who wrote in *Women, Church and State*: 'When instead of "witches" one chooses to read "women", one gains a better understanding of the cruelties inflicted by the Church on this portion of humanity.'

Mona Chollet notes, however, that contemporary feminists seem to claim to be 'witches' more than their predecessors. It has indeed taken time to get rid of the "negative images [that] continue to produce, at best, censorship or self-censorship, impediments; at worst, hostility, even violence" (p. 34).

If this began in the 1970s, notably with the creation of the magazine *Sorcières*, it is today that the feminist movement has particularly seized on this term, making the witch a real icon. Indeed, not one feminist demonstration is without its sign: "We are the granddaughters of the witches you failed to burn", not one article without reference to this character. Women thus seem to find in the witch enough strength to assume their own identity, because, as the feminist Thérèse Clerc said in 2009: "To be a witch is to be subversive of the law. It means inventing *the other law*" (p. 171).

In her essay *Witches* Mona Chollet, by explaining how the witch, eternal victim of the male moral order, has become an icon of feminism, also participates in this movement. With this book, she has become one of the most widely read feminists/witches in France.

READING KEYS

FIGURES OF THE WITCH

The single woman

Most of the women burned as witches were unmarried, because they were afraid of these women whose power was not given to them by a man in their entourage. A witch is not defined by her husband or her children. In modern times, this autonomous power is still frightening. They try to turn this fear against the women themselves, instilling in them from a very young age that to avoid marriage is to condemn oneself to live alone in sadness. But autonomy is not the absence of ties, but the possibility of choosing the ones you want.

Gloria Steinem, the sacred monster of feminism, is the most beautiful illustration of the independent woman, who led a fulfilling life on her own: writing, travelling, love, activism, etc. She gave up nothing. She gave up nothing. It was when *Newsweek* wrote about her in 1973 that it was "possible to be single and whole at the same time" (p. 45). This feminist also co-founded the monthly *Ms. Magazine*, which uses the title Ms. in its title, a 1961 invention that bears the mark of the marital status of the person it designates. In France, we will have to wait until the 21st century to question the outdated (and reactionary) "mademoiselle"…

The childless woman

Among the women who burned at the stake during the Renaissance were many healers who prevented or interrupted pregnancies. From the accusation of making children die to the accusation of not wanting them, there is only one step: 'Those who refuse motherhood are also confronted with the prejudice that they hate children, like witches devouring small roasted bodies during the Sabbath or casting a fatal spell on the neighbour's son' (p.110). Here Mona Chollet questions society's relationship to the birth rate, and the opprobrium cast on those who do not wish to have children.

Yet, the author notes, not having children can offer the woman who makes this choice a fulfilling life full of other possibilities: "giving birth to oneself, rather than passing on life; inventing a feminine identity that does away with motherhood" (p.85).

Women who do not want children are a danger to society in that they free themselves from the injunctions that weigh on women. They break the reproductive lock, claiming by their very existence that "another life as a woman is possible".

To illustrate this choice of life, Mona Chollet takes herself as an example: "In my logic, not passing on life allows for its full enjoyment. [...] This attitude makes me an embarrassing near-exception in the society I live in. In France, only 4.3 per cent of women and 6.3 per cent of men say they do not want children' (p.96). Of course, a man who does not become a father does not endanger the society he helps to shape.

Then the essayist goes further and evokes what must remain secret, what seems to be the most serious transgression, which makes a woman a monster even more than the rest: the regret of some women to have had children.

The old woman

What does the witch look like in our imagination? She has long grey hair, bushy eyebrows, a wart on her nose, and preys on young, fresh and beautiful princesses. In a word, the witch is old.

And our society, which takes the cult of youth to its extreme, has understood this. It is up to women to take up 'this absurd challenge: to pretend that time does not pass, and thus to resemble what our society considers the only acceptable form for a woman over thirty: a young girl embalmed alive' (p. 147).

And woe betide the others, as evidenced, for example, by the incomprehension and rejection faced by those who let their hair turn white, an experience recounted by Sophie Fontanel in *Une apparition*. Once again, the male counterpart does not exist. Who would think George Clooney's greying hair was out of place? For the hair that turns white is a reflection of experience, valued in men, threatening in women.

Moreover, while the experience of older women is frightening, their sexuality is totally denied. Mona Chollet illustrates her point by citing several films which, simply because they highlight the sexuality of women over 50, appear transgressive: *Une femme libre, Aurore, L'Art de vieillir...*

WITCHES, A VOICE FOR EMPOWERMENT

Empowerment is a concept that refers to the capacity to act provided by self-esteem and collective commitment.

From the very title of her book: *Sorcières. La puissance invaincue des femmes (Witches. the unconquerable power of women)*, Mona Chollet highlights the question of power. Indeed, her text clearly aims to paint a portrait of modern witches, i.e. women who accomplish themselves and not through others, especially not through men. The figure of the witch goes from being an outcast to a fighter. She is the one who speaks out, who takes back control of her body, of her life.

By reappropriating the figure of the witch, the author invites women to pass from object to subject, giving them the strength that she herself drew from the powerful women who preceded her.

"I measure the galvanising importance of identifying models", we read on page 39. Gloria Steinheim, Sophie Fontanel, Pam Houston, Corinne Maier, Barbara MacDonald, Thérèse Clerc... so many strong figures, so many ways of living in harmony with oneself, so many paths open and possibilities offered to women to come.

For each witch is "an ideal to strive for, she shows the way" (p.11), that of a woman who can hold additional power.

By speaking in the first person in this essay and referring on numerous occasions to her personal life – as a 'witch', Mona Chollet does not want children, as a 'witch', Mona Chollet has white hair – the author in turn becomes a figure to be identified with, a source from which to draw strength.

And, just as well, Mona Chollet has become with *Sorcières. La puissance invaincue des femmes* the most widely read French feminist. Her essay, released in 2018, has moreover accompanied the third feminist wave and the liberation of women's speech that exploded with the #metoo movement.

Indeed, far from limiting herself to magic and personal development advice, to which some would like to reduce the figure of the witch, the author advocates real political *empowerment*: the witch becomes the bearer of courage and will to assert herself in a man's world, or even to put it "on its head", as the last part of the text proposes.

TOWARDS ECOFEMINISM

 **ECOFEMINISM**

The term was first used by the feminist writer Françoise d'Eaubonne in her book *Feminism or Death*, published in 1974. This neologism highlights the fact that the destruction of the environment and the oppression of women are based on the same system of violence and domination. Indeed, capitalism can only exist by exploiting natural resources and the labour force used to do so.

While it is difficult to date the first manifestations of ecofeminism, it is likely that the pioneers of ecofeminism were the first victims of this system of domination, namely poor women of colour who rose up against what was destroying their land: over-industrialisation, intensive farming and ranching. Ecofeminism is therefore a cross-cutting movement.

In France, this movement was brought back to the forefront in 2021 by the candidate in the Green primary, Sandrine Rousseau, who defined herself as an ecofeminist and wanted to fight against climate change and gender inequality at the same time.

Alongside women without husbands, women without children, old women burned as witches, there were also many healers. Mona Chollet explains in her essay how, in the words of Guy Bechtel, the 'machine for making the new man' was also a 'machine for killing old women'.

Indeed, with the Cartesian discourse of the 17th century comes an arrogant, rational, all-powerful science, which accompanies the spirit of conquest of men. It was this science that signed the death warrant of the healers, who were often more competent than the official doctors.

Medicine thus becomes a male discipline, not without misogyny, which it still carries today: 'medicine still concentrates all the aspects of science born in the era of the witch-hunts: the aggressive spirit of conquest and hatred of women; the belief in the omnipotence of science and those who practise it, but also in the separation of body and mind, and in a cold rationality, devoid of all emotion' (p.197).

And reflecting further on this domestication of nature, Mona Chollet argues that it was done in conjunction with the enslavement of women, both of which were necessary for the establishment of capitalism.

Indeed, women and nature were considered dangerous in their natural state. It was therefore appropriate to put them to work by exploiting its natural resources for the former and using them as labour for the latter.

The author quotes Carolyn Merchant, an ecofeminist philosopher, who writes that 'the witch, a symbol of nature's violence, unleashed storms, caused disease, destroyed crops, prevented generation and killed young children. The woman who caused disorder, like chaotic nature, had to be brought under control' (p.191).

Ecofeminists thus want to reclaim a body that has been demonised and used for centuries. Close to nature without using it as a pretext to impose a destiny or a normed behaviour such as motherhood or heterosexuality, ecofeminists seem to be proud descendants of witches!

FOOD FOR THOUGHT

A FEW QUESTIONS TO DEEPEN YOUR REFLECTION...

- Mona Chollet published in 2021 *Reinventing Love. How patriarchy sabotages heterosexual relationships.* Do you think this theme was already present in *Sorcières*?

- Do you think that all feminists claim the term 'witch'? What might be the reasons for rejecting it?

- In her book *Sorcières*, Mona Chollet links feminism and ecology. Do you think this is relevant and why?

- If Ronsard gave a bad image of the old woman in his poem *Contre Denise sorcière*, do you know of other Baroque poems that, on the contrary, flatter the old woman?

- Mona Chollet states on page 35: "Women's independence, even when it is legally and materially possible, continues to be met with general scepticism." Do you agree with this statement?

- Chloé Delaume published *Les Sorcières de la République* in 2016. Are her witches the heirs of those who burned at the stake during the Renaissance?

- Throughout history, the term "witch hunt" has been used for other persecutions: those of communists, homosexuals, etc. What common characteristics do you see between these different persecutions?

- Pop culture (music, film, literature, etc.) is full of witch characters. Name the ones you think fit the definition given by Mona Chollet in her essay.

TO GO FURTHER

REFERENCE EDITION

CHOLLET M., *Sorcières. La puissance invaincue des femmes*, Paris, Zones, La Découverte, 2018.

BENCHMARK STUDIES

BECHTEL G., *La Sorcière et l'Occident*, Paris, Plon, 1997.

D'EUBONNE F., *Le Sexocide des sorcières*, Paris, L'Esprit frappeur, 1999.

DREURE E., « Mona Chollet, *Sorcières. La puissance invaincue des femmes* », Cahiers d'histoire. Revue d'histoire critique [Online], http://journals.openedition.org/chrhc/10208.

MICHELET J., *La Sorcière*, Paris, Flammarion, 1966.

Your opinion is important to us!
Leave a comment on the website of your online bookshop
and share your favourites on social networks!

Ebook EAN: 9782808686693
Paperback EAN: 9782808698092
Legal Deposit: D/2023/12603/1089

Cover: © Primento
Digital conception by Primento, the digital partner of publishers.